Bitty's
Halloween Surprise

A Bugleberry Book™

Written by Ruth Brook
Illustrated by Vala Kondo

Troll Associates

Library of Congress Cataloging in Publication Data

Brook, Ruth.
   Bitty's Halloween surprise.

   Summary: Betty does not join the other Bugleberries
in their excited preparations for Halloween because she
is worried about her sick cat Bitty.
   [1. Halloween—Fiction. 2. Cats—Fiction] I. Kondo,
Vala, ill. II. Title.
PZ7.B78964Bi   1988   [E]   86-30730
ISBN 0-8167-0916-5 (lib. bdg.)
ISBN 0-8167-0917-3 (pbk.)

Copyright © 1988 by Ruth Lerner Perle
Bugleberries™ is a trademark of Graymont Enterprises, Inc.
Published by Troll Associates, Mahwah, New Jersey

10   9   8   7   6   5   4   3   2   1

It was a bright autumn day in Bugleberry, and time to get ready for Halloween! The Bugleberries were on their way to Betty's house to make costumes for trick-or-treat. They laughed and played and stomped merrily through the falling leaves, making crackling sounds as they went along.

3

When they arrived, they each took out
their needles and thread, scissors and cloth,
crayons and colored markers, and went to
work.

Toony decided she would be a rag doll,
just like her own doll, Greta. Skip would be
a sailor; Rosie, a sunflower; and Dolly, a
beautiful movie star. Bo wanted to be the
greatest baseball player of all time; Jingle,
the world's greatest runner; and Baby, a
grown-up gentleman.

4

"Bitty and I are going to be a witch and
her magical cat," Betty announced. "We've
even made up a little Halloween play.
Would you like to see it?"

"Hooray, a play!" the Bugleberries
shouted. They dropped their needles and
thread, scissors and cloth, crayons and
colored markers, and stopped to watch.

7

Betty put on her witch's hat and helped Bitty on with her cape. Then she stood over a large black pot that she had placed on the table.

Frogs and newts and spiders, too.
I'll pop you in my witch's brew!

The Bugleberries stared as Betty dropped tiny plastic bugs into the pot.

Then she continued:

And when you hear the midnight bell,
My cat will cast her magic spell!

As Betty rang a little bell, Bitty jumped
onto the table and purred, "Meoooow!"
right on cue.

The Bugleberries were amazed.
"Hooray for Bitty!" they shouted.
Bitty pranced happily around
the room.

10

Soon it was time to go home. The
Bugleberries gathered their things together.
Suddenly, Dolly saw a red spot on the
rug.
"Look," said Dolly. "This looks like a
drop of blood. Did someone get cut? Is
anybody hurt?"
But nobody answered. Everyone seemed
to be fine.

The next day, the Bugleberries went back to Betty's house to finish their costumes.

When Betty opened the door, her eyes were red and teary. "Something is wrong with Bitty," she cried. "She has been hiding under the bed all day. She won't eat or drink. And when I try to come near her, she just growls."

"I'm sure she'll be better tomorrow," said Skip. "We'll go to my house and finish the costumes there. Don't get so upset! Cats can act funny at times."

But Betty knew Bitty better than that. "I think I should stay home and watch her," she said.

So the Bugleberries went off to Skip's house, leaving Betty behind.

When they came by the next day, Bitty was still no better.

"I can't come out and play," said Betty. "I have to take Bitty to the doctor."

"Oh, poo!" said Toony. "I wish you could come and play with us!"

"What a nuisance!" Jingle added. "I'm glad I don't have to worry about a pet."

"Pets are just too much trouble," said Bo.

Dolly and Lolly looked sad. "I hope Bitty feels better soon," said Dolly.

Then they all walked off to Piccolo Park
to play ball.

Betty walked in the other direction—all
the way to the animal clinic.

15

When she finally arrived, a long line of
people and pets were waiting to see the
doctor.

At last, it was Bitty's turn.

The doctor listened to Bitty's heart. He looked into her eyes and ears. He even took Bitty's temperature. Then he looked at Bitty's paw. It was very swollen and warm.

18

"Hmm," said the doctor. "It looks like Bitty cut her paw. The wound must have gotten infected. That's why she has a fever!"

He gave Bitty a shot and cleaned the wound. Then he said, "You'll have to bathe her paw in warm water and give her this medicine three times a day. If you take good care of her—and I know that you will—Bitty should be better in just a few days!"

Betty did just what the doctor said.
While the Bugleberries finished their
costumes, Betty gave Bitty her medicine.

While the Bugleberries practiced their
scariest screams for Halloween, Betty bathed
Bitty's paw.

While the Bugleberries played in Piccolo
Park, Betty tucked Bitty into her snug little
bed.

When the day was done, Betty was tired.
"Poor little kitty," she whispered to Bitty.
"You'll get better. I know you will!"
But Bitty was tired, too.
Soon they were fast asleep.

Early the next
morning, the Bugleberries
gathered at Dolly's house.
It was the day before Halloween,
but Dolly and Lolly were sad.

"What's the matter, Dolly?" asked Skip.

"Halloween won't be any fun this year if
Betty and Bitty aren't with us," she
answered.

"It's not our fault," cried Bo. "It's Bitty's.
She's just too much trouble!"

"You think pets are a lot of trouble, but
that's because you don't have a pet," said
Dolly. "If Lolly got sick, I'd stay home and
take care of her, too. She's my pet, and I
love her. She's worth all the trouble in the
world!"

"*Rrufff, rrufff!*" Lolly agreed.

The Bugleberries got very quiet. They all
felt ashamed.

24

Then they shouted, "Bugleberries to the rescue!"

And off they ran to Betty's house.

First, they washed Bitty's paw and gave her some medicine. Next, they made her little bed and covered her with a warm woolly blanket.

"If Bitty is still sick tomorrow," said Jingle, "we won't go trick-or-treating. We'll have a Halloween party here instead!"
Everyone agreed.

Halloween came, and Bitty was still not better. So the Bugleberries put on their Halloween costumes and went over to Betty's house.

Everyone took turns singing a song, telling a joke, or reciting a poem.

Then it was Betty's turn. The other Bugleberries begged her to perform her play. She said she'd try to do it without Bitty. So she sadly put on her witch's hat and stood over the large black pot on her table.

Frogs and newts and spiders, too.
I'll pop you in my witch's brew.
And when you hear the midnight bell,
My cat Bitty will be well!

Betty rang her little bell.

At the sound of the bell, Bitty looked up
from her snug little bed. She saw all the
Bugleberries smiling at her. Quick as a
wink, she jumped out of the bed and into
Betty's arms!

"Meooow!" she purred, right on cue.

"Hooray for Bitty—the star of the show!"
they all shouted.
The Bugleberries were so happy.
"Bitty is better! Bitty is better!" they
cried.

Bitty rubbed her soft furry head against
Betty's chin. It was her own special way of
saying, "Thank you for taking care of me!"
And Betty knew what she had always
known—that Bitty was worth it!
She hugged her little cat and whispered,
"This is the best Halloween ever! You're the
best, Bitty!"

32